THE MOST BRILLIANT
TRICK EVER

Will Steve's shaggy-dog trick work? Will his brother Nick fall for it? See for yourself in this very funny story.

Judy Allen has written more than fifty books – fiction and non-fiction, for adults and children. Her stories for children include *Auntie Billie's Greatest Invention*, *The Dim Thin Ducks*, *The Great Pig Sprint* and *Awaiting Developments*, which won the Whitbread Award and the Friends of the Earth Earthworm Award. She has a particular interest in ecological issues and is the author of six Animals at Risk books and the compiler of *Anthology for the Earth* (1997). She has also written two adult novels, one of which, *December Flower*, was made into a television film.

Books by the same author

The Dim Thin Ducks
The Great Pig Sprint
What is a Wall, After All?

For older readers

Awaiting Developments
The Dream Thing
Something Rare and Special

JUDY ALLEN

THE MOST BRILLIANT TRICK EVER

Illustrations by Scoular Anderson

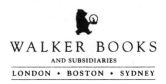

WALKER BOOKS
AND SUBSIDIARIES
LONDON • BOSTON • SYDNEY

For Tom

First published 1997 by
Walker Books Ltd, 87 Vauxhall Walk
London SE11 5HJ

This edition published 1998

2 4 6 8 10 9 7 5 3 1

Text © 1997 Judy Allen
Illustrations © 1997 Scoular Anderson

This book has been typeset in Garamond.

Printed in England

British Library Cataloguing in Publication Data
A catalogue record for this book
is available from the British Library.

ISBN 0-7445-5483-7

CONTENTS

Nick's Tricks

Steve had two parents, three stick insects, four plastic crates full of personal treasures, and one brother.

His parents were called Mum and Dad. His stick insects were called Twig, Stem and Branch. His plastic crates didn't have names. His brother was called Nick.

Nick was taller, stronger, smarter and older than Steve. He also had a weird sense of humour.

Sometimes he and Steve played together and it was fun. Other times it definitely wasn't.

One morning Steve was sitting in bed, counting his collection of football stickers. He was happy. He liked Saturdays.

Suddenly Nick burst into the room.

"What are you doing?" he yelled. "Don't you know it's Friday? You'll be late for school!"

Steve dropped his stickers all over the place, dragged on his clothes, and ran into the kitchen.

Mum was reading the Saturday newspaper.

Dad was still in bed.

Nick was staggering around the room laughing. "You *believed* it!" he snorted.

Steve glared.

"Don't get so upset," said Mum. "He's only teasing you."

That afternoon Nick told Steve he had bought a huge, savage rat from the pet shop. He had got it home all right, but it had escaped and now it was hiding under Steve's bed.

Steve spent some nasty minutes searching, with a torch in one hand and a ruler in the other.

Then he heard Nick cackling behind him.

"You *believed* it!" Nick gurgled.

"Just ignore him," said Mum. "Then he'll give up."

Two days later Nick told Steve
not to go out of the front door.

"There's a man outside who'll be
cross if you do," he said.

That time Steve *didn't* believe
him.

He opened the door, walked straight out, fell over the window cleaner's bucket and almost knocked him off his ladder.

"You should have *believed* it," said Nick.

"Try teasing him back," said Mum.

Steve's Tricks

"There's a spider on your cornflakes," said Steve to Nick the next morning.

"No, there isn't," said Nick. And there wasn't.

"We have to be in school an hour early tomorrow," said Steve, at teatime.

"No, we don't," said Nick. And they didn't.

"You'll have to do better than that," said Mum.

Steve couldn't think of anything better. He gave up and went next door to visit Mrs Blatt and Mitch. They were always pleased to see him and they never teased him.

Mrs Blatt was a human being with black hair and a nice smile. Mitch was a shaggy dog, who also had black hair and a nice smile, and such a tufty chin he looked as if he had a beard.

Mitch had several hobbies. His main ones were catching a ball in mid-air, running in the park, scratching, and playing hide-and-seek. Steve helped him with these.

Mitch's other hobbies were
burying things in the garden and
barking at motor bikes. Steve didn't
usually help him with those.

But that day when Steve went
round to Mrs Blatt's house,
something awful had happened.
Mitch had changed. He wouldn't
run or play. He didn't bark.

"I don't know what's wrong with him," said Mrs Blatt. "He's shedding more hair on the furniture than usual. And he seems depressed."

Steve was depressed, too. He went home again very soon. He forgot about tricks. All he could think of was Mitch.

Later, Steve and Nick were out
with their football when Mrs Blatt
and Mitch set off for a walk. Even
Nick noticed something wrong.

The following day when Steve went to visit Mitch …
he wasn't there.

"Mitch is at the vet's," said Mrs Blatt. "He isn't well."

"When is he coming back?" said Steve.

"I'm not sure," said Mrs Blatt.

Steve hurried home to tell his parents.

He isn't well.

She's very worried about Mitch.

"I know," said Mum. "Steve, don't ask Mrs Blatt too many questions. You'll upset her. She's very worried about Mitch."

"So am I," said Steve.

"Luckily, Mrs Blatt's son is coming to stay with her for a few days," said Mum. "He'll cheer her up."

"Will Mitch get better?" said Steve.

"I hope so," said Mum. "He's more than just a dog to Mrs Blatt. Really he's almost human."

Steve could have had his brilliant idea right then. But he didn't, quite. He didn't get it until next day when he went next door.

He wasn't planning to ask about Mitch. He didn't want to upset Mrs Blatt. He just thought that if he stood quietly in her kitchen, she might talk to him about Mitch anyway.

When he got there, he found that
Mrs Blatt was not alone. There was
a man in her kitchen. A tall man
with shaggy black hair, a nice smile,
and a beard. He looked quite like
Mrs Blatt – apart from the beard.

He also looked quite like Mitch – including the beard. He was Mrs Blatt's son.

And *that* was when Steve thought of it.

NICK TRICKED

Steve stayed just long enough to hear Mrs Blatt telling him that Mitch was still at the vet's, but getting better.

Then he ran home, thinking hard.

Had his brother heard Mum say Mrs Blatt's son was coming to visit? No, he hadn't. He hadn't been in the room when she'd said that. Did Nick know Mitch was at the vet's? No, he didn't. He hadn't been in the room when Mum had talked about that, either.

Steve ran indoors, shouting.

"Nick! Nick! Mitch has turned into a human."

"No, he hasn't," said Nick.

That didn't bother Steve. He hadn't expected the trick to work right away.

"He has!" he said. "Remember he went all quiet and his hair was coming out? That was the start of it."

"Rubbish," said Nick, but he was beginning to look interested.

"You watch their door," said Steve. "He has to come out sometime."

Nick just shrugged. But he did watch the Blatts' door. And after a while Mr Blatt did come out.

Steve could hardly believe his luck. Mr Blatt was wearing running shorts and a vest. He waved to the boys, danced about on his toes for a few moments, and then set off along the pavement.

Steve grabbed Nick's arm.

"See!" he said, as Mr Blatt trotted away from them. "Same hair! Same beard! And he still likes running!"

"I don't believe it," said Nick. But he didn't sound absolutely sure.

Steve and Nick stood side by side and watched as Mr Blatt sprinted to the end of the street. Then, just as he was about to step off the pavement, a motor bike roared past, right in front of his nose. Mr Blatt stood still and shouted after it.

FOOL! You're going too fast!

"See!" said Steve, really excited now. "Mitch always shouted at motor bikes. You know he did!"

"I don't believe it," said Nick again. But he was beginning to.

NICK BELIEVES

Next day, Steve's mother told the boys to smarten themselves up. The family was to have Sunday lunch at Mrs Blatt's.

When they arrived, Mrs Blatt asked the grown-ups to sit down and shooed the boys out into the garden.

"It's a nice day," she said, "and lunch won't be ready for half an hour."

Mr Blatt was already out there. He had his back turned and he was busy digging. He didn't notice them straight away.

"Look," said Steve, quietly. "He's *burying* something. Just like he always did."

"Mitch didn't use a spade," Nick muttered. He tried hard to sound scornful, but he failed.

"He couldn't when he was a dog," said Steve. "He didn't have hands."

Mr Blatt heard them and turned round.

Hello there!

"Like a game before lunch?" he said. He picked up a ball and threw it to Nick. Nick was so startled he almost didn't catch it.

Whenever he could take his eyes off the flying ball, Steve looked at Nick. And he saw what he hoped to see. It was working better than he had dreamed. Nick was definitely beginning to believe it.

Then Mrs Blatt called them in to
lunch and planted a huge dish in
the middle of the table.

"I've cooked his favourite,"
she said, beaming at Mr Blatt.
"Spare ribs!"

"Delicious!" said Mum.

"Terrific!" said Dad.

"Grrrrrreat!"
growled
Mr Blatt, and
he seized
one of the
ribs in both
hands and
began to
gnaw on it.

That did it.

"Do you believe it now?" Steve whispered to Nick.

"I *believe* it," Nick whispered back.

That should have been Steve's big moment. He should have felt triumphant. Instead he found he had a funny feeling in his stomach.

Mr Blatt really did look very much like Mitch, especially when he was enjoying his spare ribs. What if the trick he had thought he was playing on Nick turned out to be true? What if Mitch really had turned into this hairy, bearded man!

Nick Tells

On Monday, Nick told his gang at
school about the dog that had turned
into a man. He also told them they
must keep the story secret.

Mrs Blatt must be a witch, he said, and she'd probably be angry if they gave her away. No one knew what awful things an angry witch could do. No one *wanted* to know.

Two of them believed him, three of them half-believed him and one of them didn't believe him at all. But they all wanted to see Mr Mitch Blatt.

So after school they gathered
around the Blatts' front gate. They
let Steve come with them, even
though he was younger. They said
they had a job for him.

Steve's job was to go into the
house and keep Mrs Blatt talking so
she wouldn't notice them hanging
around and chase them away.

Steve went into the kitchen.
Mrs Blatt smiled at him. If she was
a witch, he thought, then she was a
very kind witch.

"Mrs Blatt," he said, without really
meaning to, "can Mitch be changed
back again?"

Mrs Blatt...

Mrs Blatt was in the middle of tidying away some saucepans. She was making such a clatter that she didn't hear exactly what he said.

"Oh, yes," she said, smiling even more. "Mitch is coming back today. He's well again. My son has just

Oh, yes!

gone to fetch him. Let's go and
watch for them from the front
window!"

Steve was so happy to hear that
Mitch really was still a dog that he
forgot his job. He forgot he was
supposed to stop Mrs Blatt looking
out and seeing Nick's gang.

TEAM WORK

Steve remembered his job when he
saw Nick and the others glaring
at him over the gate. Then he forgot
again, because there was Mr Blatt,
beaming all over his beard, striding
towards the house, with Mitch
bounding beside him.

"Those two are very alike, aren't they?" laughed Mrs Blatt as she and Steve hurried out of the front door.

They all met on the garden path and Mitch and Mrs Blatt fell into each other's arms.

Next to Mrs Blatt, though, Mitch
loved Steve, and he greeted him
enthusiastically.

Suddenly, in the middle of all the
excitement, Steve thought of his
brother.

Nick was standing by himself on the pavement, looking white. His gang were all in a group, facing him. Two of them were actually pointing at him.

"It was just a joke," Nick was saying, feebly.

"You weren't playing a joke," they said. "You *believed* it!"

Nick had been looking white. Now he began to go red. There was a serious danger that he might cry. Steve suddenly felt very grown up. He walked over and stood beside his brother.

"Hey, Nick," he said. "Our trick worked, didn't it?"

Nick looked surprised.

The other boys looked uncertain.

"It was the most brilliant trick ever!" said Steve. "We really fooled them!"

Nick began to grin.

We really fooled them!

"Yes, we really *did* fool them," he said. The others shrugged and tried to look super-cool.

"It was *quite* a good joke," said one.

"Not bad," said another.

"OK, I suppose," said a third.

Then they all went home.

As soon as they were too far away to hear, Steve danced around in front of Nick. "I *did* it!" he said. "I *got* you! You *believed* it."

Nick started to shake his head. Then he stopped.

"Yes," he said. "I did. You were brilliant. Can you think of any more as good as that?"

"Maybe," said Steve.

"I'll help you," said Nick. "We could make a great team!"